P is for Pumpkin

Written by
Kathy-jo Wargin

Illustrated by
YaWen Ariel Pang

ZONDERkidz

ZONDERVAN.com/
AUTHORTRACKER
follow your favorite authors

Apples and Acorns and all sorts of things—
Let's find the blessings that God's autumn brings.

A is for Apple

It brings the **B**arn dance where good friends all meet
to share in God's Word and good food to eat.

B is for Barn

Let's try the **C**orn maze—which way should we go?
Turn right and turn left into each crazy row.

CORN

ENTER

Maze

C is for Corn

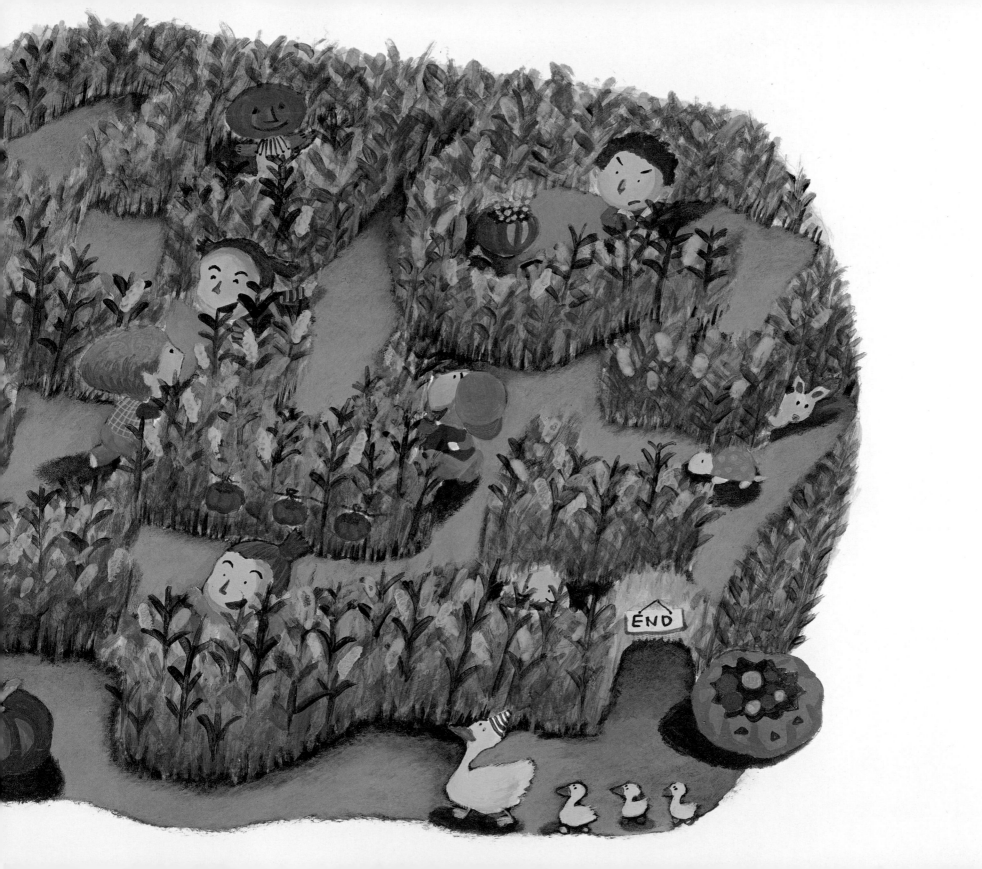

Autumn means **D**ress-up, but who will I be?
If I wear a mask, God still knows it's me!

D is for Dress-up

For God made the **E**arth—he made everything!
He makes all the wonders each season will bring.

E is for Earth

He changes the colors on leaves big and small,
red, brown, and yellow to tell us it's **F**all.

F is for Fall

He turns the fields into ribbons of **G**old,
sparkling with frost as the autumn grows cold.

G is for Gold

The **H**arvest brings baskets filled up to the brim,
with corn, beans, and squash—all gifts from him!

H is for Harvest

The **I**ndian corn with colorful rows
is perfect for drying and hanging with bows.

I is for Indian Corn

The bright **J**ack-o'-lantern with its friendly, big grin
reminds us God's love is a light from within.

J *is for Jack-o'-lantern*

Fill up the kettles with warm soup to share!
Autumn brings **K**indness and neighbors who care.

K is for Kindness

Autumn brings **L**eaves, so let's grab a rake
and jump up and down in the piles we make.

L is for Leaves

One sign of autumn is harvest **M**oon's light,
God's gentle blessing for this autumn night.

M is for Moon

We can spend time on a long **N**ature walk.
If we listen closely, we might hear God talk.

N is for Nature

Autumn means **O**rchards with apples for pie.
Let's pick the ripe ones—would you like to try?

O is for Orchards

When autumn is here we pick **P**umpkins too.
I'll find the biggest and give it to you!

P is for Pumpkin

Now peek in the church—what do you see?
Sewing and laughing at the Quilting bee!

Q is for Quilting Bee

Ravens are flying in the fall sky,
black against orange as each one floats by ...

R is for Ravens

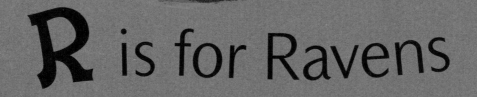

...over the **S**carecrow, all stuffed with hay.
A reminder that God watches us each day.

S is for Scarecrow

T is for Trick or Treat

This time of year children say "Trick or Treat!"
or go to their churches for fun things to eat.

In autumn, the **U**niverse fills with great things,
like birds flying south on strong, silent wings.

U is for Universe

Just look in the sky and you will sure see
the geese flying south in a big letter V!

Birds fly in a big letter V

The horses are waiting; the trail's long and wide.
The hay **W**agon's ready. Let's go for a ride!

W is for Wagon

Laughing and singing for eXtra big fun,
sitting on hay bales until the ride's done.

X is for eXtra big fun

Beyond **Y**ellow fields at the end of the day,
we watch the sun as it slips far away.

Zip up your jacket and I'll zip mine too.
It's time to go home; the autumn day's through.

Y is for Yellow • **Z** is for Zip

From Apples and Acorns
and other great things,
may you find every blessing
that God's autumn brings.

To Jake. May every autumn be beautiful.
K.J.W.

For my parents.
May God bless you and keep you healthy.
Y.A.P.

ZONDERKIDZ

P is for Pumpkin
Copyright © 2008 by Kathy-jo Wargin
Illustrations © 2008 by YaWen Ariel Pang

Requests for information should be addressed to:
Zonderkidz, *Grand Rapids, Michigan 49530*

This edition: ISBN 978-0-310-72635-7 (softcover)

Library of Congress Cataloging-in-Publication Data

Wargin, Kathy-jo.
    P is for pumpkin / by Kathy-jo Wargin ; illustrated by YaWen Ariel Pang.
        p. cm.
        Summary: Presents rhyming sentences for each letter of the alphabet that
    remind the reader of God's blessings in autumn.
        ISBN 978-0-310-71180-3 (hardcovercover)
        [1. Autumn—Fiction. 2. God—Fiction. 3. Alphabet. 4. Stories in rhyme.]
    I. Pang, Ariel, ill. II. Title.
    PZ8.3.W2172Paai 2008
    [E]—dc22   2006014791

All Scripture quotations unless otherwise indicated are taken from the Holy Bible,
New International Version®, *NIV*®. Copyright © 1973, 1978, 1984, 2011 by Biblica,
Inc.™ Used by permission. All rights reserved worldwide.

Editors: Bruce Nuffer & Betsy Flikkema
Art direction & design: Laura Maitner-Mason

Printed in China

14 15 16 17 /LPC/ 9 8 7 6 5 4 3